"You know, tomorrow we can't fool around," I said. "We've got to keep our heads in the game."

Butter said, "Brad, I think I'll keep my head in my baseball cap." I tried not to laugh. Dad always says I have to be serious about baseball. He wants me to be really good. But sometimes he acts as if he wants me to be the best player in the world right now—before I turn nine.

For Michael Russell and Steven Hughes,
my grandsons
—D.H.

Thanks to Brett and Jessica
—L.J.

Text copyright © 1998 by Dean Hughes.
Illustrations copyright © 1998 by Layne Johnson.
All rights reserved under International and Pan-American Copyright Conventions.
Published in the United States by Random House, Inc., New York, and simultaneously in Canada by Random House of Canada Limited, Toronto.

http://www.randomhouse.com/

Library of Congress Cataloging-in-Publication Data
Hughes, Dean, 1943–
Brad and Butter play ball! / by Dean Hughes ; illustrated by Layne Johnson.
    p.   cm.
"A Stepping Stone book."
SUMMARY: Eight-year-old Brad tries to follow his father's advice so he can be a good baseball player, but his best friend, Warren, a.k.a. "Butter," is the one who helps him with his game.
ISBN 0-679-88355-X (pbk.) — ISBN 0-679-98355-4 (lib. bdg.)
[1. Baseball—Fiction.   2. Friendship—Fiction.   3. Fathers and sons—Fiction.]
I. Johnson, Layne, ill.   II. Title.   PZ7.H87312Br   1998   [Fic]—dc21   97-18051

Printed in the United States of America   10 9 8 7 6 5 4 3 2 1

A STEPPING STONE BOOK is a registered trademark of Random House, Inc.

Brad and Butter
Play Ball!

by Dean Hughes

illustrated by
Layne Johnson

A STEPPING STONE BOOK™

Random House ⌂ New York

Butter is my best friend. We've been buddies since we were little kids.

There was the time our kindergarten teacher, Ms. Larsen, told us that she was getting married. So Butter started kissing his arm to make smooching noises.

I tried not to laugh. But Butter laughs like a train—*chug, chug, chug, chug.* When he starts laughing, so do I. Then neither one of us can stop.

We both got in trouble that day. But that's when we got to be best friends.

Now Butter and I are in the third grade. We're not in the same class, but we're on the same baseball team. It's called the Rug Bugs.

Yeah, I know. I don't like that name either.

But the guy who buys the uniforms owns a rug store. Hal's Carpet and Floor Coverings. His name is Hal.

I wanted to be the Rug Rats, but Hal said, "That doesn't rhyme." I don't see why that matters.

On the night before our first game, I called Butter. His real name is Warren, but when his little brother tries to say "brother," he says "Butta."

That's how Butter got to be Butter.

Butter's little brother is named

William. But Butter calls him "Bother," which is a good name for him!

I asked Butter if he was excited. He said, "Sure."

So I asked him if he had all his stuff ready.

"I have my hat and my shirt," he said.

"Aren't you going to get wristbands?" I asked him.

Butter said, "Wristbands? What are they for?"

"I don't know," I told him. "But me and my dad just got back from the mall. And my dad got me some. So we must need them."

Butter said, "Maybe they're to keep your hands from falling off." *Chug, chug, chug, chug.*

Then I said, "Maybe we could use them for slingshots."

"Coach Moosman could use them to hold his pants up," Butter said.

"Yeah. If he'd pull his pants up higher, we wouldn't have to look at his hairy belly button."

Butter really chugged at that one.

I was laughing, too, but I told Butter, "You know, tomorrow we can't fool around. We've got to keep our heads in the game."

Butter said, "I think I'll keep my head in my baseball cap."

I tried not to laugh that time. Dad always says I have to be serious about baseball. He wants me to be really good. Like maybe the greatest player in the world.

That's what I want, too. I want to be a shortstop in the major leagues. And hit *lonnnnnggg* dingers.

That's what me and Butter call home runs.

But sometimes Dad makes me nervous. He acts as if he wants me to be the best player in the world right now—before I turn nine.

Lately, the only thing he talks about is baseball. He tells me I've got to believe in myself and always give 110 percent. Stuff like that. Half the time I don't even know what he means.

Angela, my smart-aleck little sister, always says, "Brad can't even hit the ball. I know. I've watched him."

Dad tells her, "I don't want to hear you talk that way." And he means it.

I'm glad he says that. I just worry that I might mess up and he'll be disappointed. But Dad's a good dad. Benny Schmetzer's dad wears bow ties and shiny white shoes.

He doesn't know beans about sports. My dad was a star player in college. He knows everything.

And he's fun sometimes. He knows how to act like a frog—he pretends to catch flies with his tongue. He even makes frog noises.

When we went to the mall, Dad bought me a new glove. And we got everything else I needed: sneakers, batting gloves, three new balls. And those wristbands.

I went home and tried on all my new stuff. And I put my Rug Bugs shirt on. Boy, did I look cool.

Dad saw me, and he said, "You look like a real ballplayer."

But Mom said, "I hope you have fun. That's the important thing."

"The way to have fun is to be a great

player," said Dad. And then he took me outside so we could practice a little.

I had been working out with my team, but Dad likes to give me some extra pointers.

When we got outside, he said, "Show me your stance again."

I tried to stand the way he told me before.

Dad said, "Okay. That's not bad. But keep your feet closer together. Hold your bat higher. Put more weight on your back foot. Lean toward the plate. And look right at me."

I tried to do all that stuff. But I felt as if I was going to fall on my face.

Then he pitched the ball.

I swung at it, but I missed.

"Don't wiggle your bat around," Dad said. "Hold it steady."

I tried to remember that. Plus all the other stuff. But I was all mixed up. Did I have to hold my feet higher? Or hold my bat closer? Or lean on my back foot?

I swung and missed about twenty times.

Dad finally said, "Okay, you're doing better. But you have to take a level swing."

How could I swing level? *I* wasn't level.

But I didn't say that. I just thought about my feet and my hands and my head—and I swung as level as I could.

But I tripped and almost fell down.

That's when Dad said, "Brad, you're just nervous. You'll come through when the game starts. That's what I always did."

I sure hoped he was right. But about a thousand people were going to be staring at me at the game. What if I fell on my face, right on home plate?

On the way to the game, I was so scared I couldn't sit still. Mom kept saying, "It's okay, Brad. Just relax."

But I was twisting around and I accidentally kicked Angela. She slugged me in the shoulder. Then she said, "I think Brad's got ants in his pants. He's going to play *terrible*."

"He'll do just fine," Dad said. But I saw his eyes in the rear-view mirror. He looked worried.

My stomach was doing weird stuff. It felt as if squirrels were inside me, chasing each other in circles.

When we got to the field, Joey Duden walked up to me. He's the second biggest guy on our team. I'm just lucky Butter is the biggest.

"Forget about playing shortstop," he said. "That's what *I'm* going to play." He was standing really close. "You're a *stinking* player. Your name should be *Stinkle*, not Hinkle."

"You stink more than I do, Duden," I said. I thought about calling him "Doo-Doo." Then I decided I better not.

"Oh, yeah? Say that again and I'll step on your tongue," Joey said.

After that, I didn't feel like talking to him anymore.

Most of the other players were acting

hyper. We all had our brown Rug Bugs shirts on. Andy Tolman's hung down below his knees. It looked like a dress. Boy, I felt sorry for him. Mine was too big, but not *that much* too big.

Everyone was there except Butter. That worried me. Sometimes he forgets

things. His mom does, too. But finally I saw Butter and Bother and their mom walking across the park.

I could see that Butter was way too big for his shirt. RUG BUGS was all stretched out. But the worst thing was, his belly was showing—just like Coach Moosman's.

At least Butter didn't have hair on his stomach. Coach Moosman's bellybutton looks like a big hairy cave. It's really gross-looking.

But Butter looked almost as bad. I could see his knobby bellybutton, all bare naked. He's got an "outie," not an "innie" like the coach.

"My shirt's kind of small for me," Butter said. Then he turned around and bent over. There was a big space between his shirt and his jeans. I don't want to tell you what I saw—but it looked like the Grand Canyon.

Butter's mother is a big lady with curly red hair that sticks out in all directions. She saw what I saw, and she started making little squeaky sounds. That's how she laughs.

Bother said, "I can see your cwack,

Butta." Then he about fell down from laughing.

I was laughing, too. I couldn't help it.

Coach Moosman didn't laugh. He started looking in his equipment bag. He found a shirt that fit Butter better.

The only trouble was, it had COACH on it. But Butter didn't care.

After that, I told Butter what Joey had been saying to me. And how I almost called him "Joey Doo-Doo."

Butter grinned. Then he said, "I'll call him 'Doggy-Doo Duden' if he messes with you again."

Before the game started, the coach had all of us kids sit on the grass. Then he talked to us.

My dad stood right behind me and Butter. A couple of times he said, "That's right, Brad. Remember that."

One thing the coach told us was: "If you hit the ball, run to that base over there." He pointed to first base. Then he asked Carl Brickey, "Have you got that now?"

In practice, Carl always hit the ball and ran to third. Every time. He's left-handed.

Then the coach told us, "On grounders, keep your glove on the ground. And keep your fanny down."

Some of the kids giggled about that.

Butter whispered to me, "If I do that, I might lose my pants. You better give me those wristbands."

I started smiling, but I didn't dare laugh. Dad would have heard me.

"And another thing," the coach said. "Us coaches do the pitching. But don't swing at every pitch. Wait for a good one."

"How do you know if it's a good one?"

Michael Storberg said.

"It'll be in the strike zone," the coach told him. "Do you know where that is?"

Michael said, "Over by home plate, I think."

Butter started chugging again. "I hope Michael doesn't bump into the strike zone and get hurt," he said.

I tried like crazy not to laugh.

Then Gwennie Sanderson said, "Hey, Coach, I don't like these shirts. How come we have to be the Rug Bugs?"

"That's the name Hal likes," the coach said. "The guy who buys the shirts gets to pick the name."

"Nuh-uh," Gwennie said. "We're the ones who have to wear the stupid things. I wish they were baby blue."

Sherry Alvarez said, "Yeah, and Rug Bugs is a rotten name. Me and Gwennie thought up a better one: the Diamond Stars."

Oh, brother. I couldn't believe it.

I whispered to Butter, "We can't be that. We have to be something that sounds *mean*."

"Yeah. Like the Killer Guppies."

That got me laughing. And it got Butter chugging.

My dad said, "Brad, pay attention. You too, Butter."

I told myself Dad was right. I had better get my head in the game if I wanted to play all right.

But as soon as I thought about that, those squirrels in my stomach went wild again.

And I needed to go to the bathroom. Bad.

We were playing against the All-Purpose Muffler Shop Rumbles. They didn't look like they were very good.

But we didn't look so great either. Especially Butter (wearing a coach's shirt) and Andy (practically with a dress on).

Jeremy Nash, our catcher, was our first batter. He struck out. But I wasn't surprised. His stance was all wrong.

Teddy Kinski was up second. I was on deck. That meant I could go out and swing my bat and get warmed up.

I tried to think about hitting home runs. Long dingers. But I felt like those squirrels had climbed into my head.

Teddy swung at the first pitch. And he hit it! Sort of. It rolled slowly toward first base.

The first baseman ran up to get it. But he didn't keep his glove down. Or his fanny. The ball rolled through his legs.

So the pitcher ran over and grabbed the ball. And he threw it to first base. But no one was there. The ball went flying out to right field.

Teddy ran to second and stopped. The coach yelled, "Keep going, Teddy! Keep going! Run to third!"

But Teddy stayed at second base.

"Run to third!" the coach yelled again.

But Teddy said, "I'm too tired."

I looked at Butter. He had come out on deck. I told him, "If the coach tells you something, you have to do it."

"Maybe Teddy doesn't know where third is," Butter said. And he started to chug.

But I couldn't laugh. I was up next. I had to concentrate.

When I got in the batter's box, I tried to remember everything. I got my feet right. And my head. My hands. My shoulders. Every part of me.

When I felt like I was going to fall down, I was ready.

The first pitch was a bad one—low. I didn't swing.

"Good eye, Brad," Coach Moosman yelled.

Whew! But then I had to think about all my body parts again.

The next pitch was a good one. I swung, but I missed.

My dad yelled, "Keep your eye on the ball, Brad!"

So *that* was what I had done wrong. The next pitch was a beauty. I kept my eye on the ball and I swung as hard as I could.

But I missed.

Coach Moosman yelled, "Don't try to kill the ball!"

The Rumbles infielders were yelling, "Hey, batta, batta. My grandma can hit better than you." Stuff like that.

I tried not to listen. I got back into my stance. "Don't try to kill it," I whispered.

I swung nice and easy—and missed.

"Strike three. You're out!" the umpire said.

I already knew that. I know all the rules of baseball.

Coach Moosman yelled, "That's all right, Brad!"

And then my mom said, really loud, "Don't feel bad, honey."

I wish she wouldn't call me that. Not in front of all the guys.

When I walked into the dugout, Jesse Putnam and Albert Farnbach were having a burping contest. Gwennie kept saying, "You guys are *sick*-ening."

Joey said, "I knew you wouldn't get a hit, *Stinkle*."

"Let's see *you* do any better," I told him.

Then I sat on the bench. I was mad at Joey, but mostly I was wondering what my dad was thinking. I didn't look toward the bleachers.

Butter was up next. I was worried he would strike out, too. He stepped up to home plate. Then he just stood there. He didn't even have a stance.

The first pitch was a bad one. If Butter hadn't swung, the coach would have said, "Good eye."

Butter swung anyway.

And he hit the ball.

It went about a mile, too.

Everyone on the Rumbles chased after it, but it rolled under a bush.

I started jumping up and down and yelling, "Run hard, Butter. Run hard!" Poor Butter can't run very fast. But he made it all the way around the bases for a home run.

I ran out to home plate, and I gave him a high five. He was grinning really big. "I got me a dinger," he said.

When he got back to the dugout, even Jesse and Albert stopped burping long enough to give him high fives.

Butter had been pretty lucky. But I was still worried. He didn't have a good eye.

Right after that, my dad came down to the dugout. He talked to me through the wire fence. He said, "Brad, you forgot what I told you."

"I got mixed up," I said.

"Why were you so bent over?"

"I thought that's what you said to do."

"No, not at all. Now listen closely. Next time, hold your bat still. Keep your weight on your back foot, but don't lean so much. Lift your front foot and stride forward. Swing level. And don't try to kill the ball."

"Okay," I said. But I was already forgetting.

Dad walked back to the bleachers. Butter said, "He's right. We don't need any dead balls around here."

"Be quiet a sec," I said. "I'm trying to remember all that stuff. What did he say? I have to keep my back foot—"

"You must be a dog if you have back feet. My feet are next to each other."

"Come on, Butter," I said. "Don't mess around. What did he say about lifting my foot?"

"Don't do that, Brad! You know what a dog does when he lifts his leg."

Oh, brother. I couldn't remember anything. And now Butter had me laughing again.

4

Most of the kids on our team got hits after that. Sort of.

Nobody hit the ball very far. But the Rumbles threw it all over the place.

Gwennie sort of hit a triple.

She barely ticked the ball. It dropped in front of home plate. The Rumbles' catcher said it wasn't a fair ball. While he argued with the umpire, Gwennie kept running—all the way to third.

When I got up again, it was still the first inning. By then, we already had eight runs.

And this time I was ready. I wanted to hit a home run—just like Butter. I got in my stance. And I stood mostly on one foot. My back one, I think.

When I saw the ball coming, I took a step.

I tried to swing level, too. But I was falling over.

I didn't kill the ball. That's for sure.

I missed.

Three times.

The inning was over, and I had made two of the outs.

This time Joey said, "Even Carl Brickey is better than you. At least he hits the ball before he runs to the wrong base."

It was our turn in the field. Coach told

me to play shortstop. And he told Joey to play right field. Joey was mad—and I was glad.

The first guy up for the Rumbles hit a slow grounder. It rolled onto the grass and stopped. No one knew who was supposed to go after it.

So no one did.

The batter made it to first. And Coach Moosman got mad.

"Go get the ball," he said. "Don't stand around scratching your behinds."

But I wasn't scratching my behind. I just didn't know what to do.

"Take the force-out at second this time," the coach yelled.

Half the kids on our team probably don't know what a force-out is. But I do.

The next Rumbles guy didn't hit the ball very far either. But I ran after it, got my fanny down, and I grabbed it. Then I threw to second.

But the guy from first was already standing on second by then.

Coach Moosman said, "Brad, you should have gone to first with that one. You had a better chance."

"You said to make a force-out," I told him.

"I know," he said. Now he was scratching *his* behind. "But sometimes you have to decide what's best. That's something you'll learn."

"Okay," I told him. But I didn't know what he was talking about.

After that, a Rumbles guy struck out. Then they got some hits—sort of—and got three runs. Then another kid struck out.

Two away.

The next guy hit a ball that bounced right at Butter, who was playing first base.

Butter made a big mistake. He didn't get his fanny down at all! He just reached down and grabbed the ball.

And he stepped on first before the batter got there.

I couldn't believe how lucky he was. But he still needed to do things right.

When Butter was up to bat in the next inning, he didn't have a good eye again. He swung at a high pitch.

But he got another hit. A triple.

Butter's mom started making sounds like an ambulance. "Waaaayyyyyy to gooooooooo, Warrrrrrrren."

And Bother was yelling, "Yay, Butta! Yay, Butta!"

When Jesse got a hit, Butter scored another run. When he came back to the dugout, he said, "I'm tired. I have to run too far every time."

He was really sweating.

"I wish I could hit a triple," I told Butter.

He said, "Hit one, then. Just give the ball a whack—and run hard."

Yeah, I wish.

The next time I got up, the coach called time out. He called me over. He said, "Brad, what are you trying to do when you're up to bat? You look like a pretzel."

"My dad taught me a good stance," I said.

"Well…yeah," he said. "But stand up straighter. Get your balance. Step toward the pitcher, not toward the plate."

"Oh. Okay," I told him.

Now I knew what I had been doing wrong. Dad had told me to step, but he hadn't said *where*.

So now I was ready. But I can't figure out what happened. I struck out again.

And Joey called me a doofus.

"You struck out, too," I told him.

He said, "At least I didn't look like a doofus, *Stinkle*."

"You looked like a *double* doofus, *Doo-Doo*."

Then he said he was going to knock my head for a home run. And I told him, "Just try it."

But my dad started yelling. He said to get my head in the game.

And he was right. I started thinking about the game. Not about fighting with Joey.

But after that the coach told Joey to play shortstop. And he sent me to right field. That's where the worst players always have to go. I didn't want to play there.

But at least Joey wasn't a good short-stop. He made some errors.

That guy is a doofus, if you ask me. A *triple* doofus. A *doo-doo* doofus.

We won the game by about twenty runs. Butter was the star. But I finally hit a home run, too.

I ticked the ball and it rolled onto the grass. But the Rumbles catcher threw it over the first baseman's head.

And the right fielder threw it over the second baseman's head.

And the left fielder threw it over his own head. Straight up. I think it slipped out of his hand.

By the time they were finished, I had run around all the bases.

And I jumped on home plate.

Then I threw my fists in the air. Just like the big-league guys do. Butter grabbed me and just about broke my ribs.

"You hit a dinger!" he yelled. "Way to go, Brad!"

My mom was yelling, "You did it, honey! You did it!"

Even Angela was yelling for me.

But Joey said, "That wasn't a homer. That was a *ticker*."

"It was a ticker-homer," Butter said. *Chug, chug, chug.* "That's the hardest kind."

After the game, Dad said, "You did fine, Brad." But then he started talking about my back foot and my front foot again.

I could tell he didn't think I'd played very well.

When I got home, I went to my room. I felt bad about striking out so much. And only hitting a ticker for a homer.

But I figured out what to do.

I got on my bike and I went to the library. I checked out three books on baseball.

I read about stance and a good eye. And about catching and throwing and fielding.

Now I knew *everything* about baseball. Before, I sort of knew everything. But now I really did.

So I went out in the backyard with my bat. And I made a baseball diamond.

Spot's dish was home plate.

A Frisbee was first base.

The pear tree, second.

And a brown spot in the lawn, third.
(My dog made the spot. He's all one
color. Brown. But we call him Spot—
because of what he makes on our lawn.)

I didn't have a pitcher to throw to me.
I just practiced everything in my mind.

It was the seventh game of the World
Series. Two outs in the bottom of the
ninth. I was the shortstop for the New

York Yankees. And right now I was up to bat.

A guy on our team was on base, but we were behind by one run. That's when I hit the ball clear out of the yard, I mean stadium.

Then I ran around the bases with my elbows stuck out wide.

The crowd cheered like crazy.

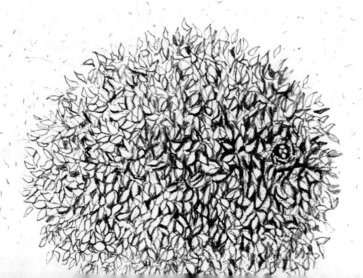

Or sometimes, I'd hit a line drive, and then slide into second for a double.

You can't believe how many hits I got. I was *smashing* the ball every time. I knocked so many homers I had to run around the bases about a hundred times.

I didn't mind running so far, either. I have a good attitude. The books said that you have to have a good attitude.

I knew I'd play better in the next game.

But at practice the next day, Coach Moosman pitched to me. And I didn't smash the ball. Mostly, I still swung and missed. At least I hit a few good ones.

When I played shortstop, I had some more trouble. When I threw the ball hard enough, it went crooked. When I threw straight, the ball didn't make it all the way to first.

I don't think Joey was any better. But he said to me, "I bet I'll be the shortstop from now on, *Stinkle*. You can't even throw right."

The coach heard us arguing and said, "Hey, you two, that's enough of that. Team members *support* each other."

That's what the books said, too. So I decided I wouldn't fight with Joey anymore.

But Joey didn't decide the same thing. He whispered, "Carl will get to play in the next game. *You'll* be the benchwarmer."

After practice, I rode home on my bike with Butter. I asked him if I would be a benchwarmer, like Joey said.

Butter said, "If the coach makes you a benchwarmer, I'll be one, too."

"You can't," I said. "You're the star of the team."

"I don't think so," he said. "You know a lot more about baseball than I do."

Butter was right about that. So I told him, "I have some books that tell you about a good stance and all that stuff."

But Butter said, "Do the books say you have to bat like a dog—and lift your back leg?" *Chug, chug, chug.*

"It's not like a dog," I said. Then I tried to explain about striding forward and all the things I had read about.

But Butter told me, "Brad, you worry too much. I just look at the ball and *whack* it. That's what you ought to do."

"Do you think I could?"

"Sure. It's easy."

I wondered if that was what I should do. That night Dad practiced with me some more. Finally, I told him that my stance made me feel like I was falling down.

He said, "It may feel a little strange at first. But if you learn good habits, you'll start hitting before long."

That sounded right. I decided I had better do what he said.

"And, Brad, you have to give one hundred and ten percent all the time. You have to *concentrate*. That's what the great players do."

That sounded right, too.

But when I went to bed that night, my mom kissed me and tucked the sheet around me. Then she said, "Honey, don't worry so much about baseball."

That was the same thing Butter said.

I didn't know *who* was right.

6

Our next game was against the Clean-as-a-Whistle Janitor Service Sweepers. They were pretty good. They scored seven runs in the first inning.

Joey was wrong. I wasn't a bench-warmer. I played shortstop again.

The Sweepers mostly got runs when we made mistakes. The biggest one was when Teddy Kinski left to go to the bathroom and didn't tell anyone. When a Sweeper hit the ball to left field, no one was there.

When the Rug Bugs got up, we scored nine runs.

But I struck out.

Twice.

I couldn't figure it out. I did every single thing those books said. And what my dad said, too.

I kept my feet as far apart as my shoulders. (Except I'm not sure if my shoulders were apart.)

I leaned forward. (But I didn't twist up like a pretzel.)

I put my weight on my back foot. (That's the one in the back of the batter's box, closest to the catcher. It's not like a dog's back feet.)

I turned my chin forward so that it was touching my shoulder. (And almost broke my neck.)

And I tried to relax. (But I didn't do so well at that.)

I took three good swings each time. And I only fell down once.

But I missed all six pitches. I didn't even get a ticker.

Joey laughed at me both times. I almost told him to shut up. But the books said to be a good sport—and not say stuff like that.

So I said, "You better read some baseball books, Joey. You're not supposed to *criticize* guys on your own team."

Joey is about the worst sport I ever met. He gave me a shove. Then he said, "Watch out or I'll *criticize* you right in the nose."

The coach told *us* to lay off. As if it was my fault.

And Dad came down to the dugout

and told me, "Brad, I want you to stop all this nonsense."

I said, "Joey started it."

That got him mad. "You straighten up or I'll take you home," he said. "Team members should *never* argue with each other."

I started to tell him I knew that. From the books. But he went back to the bleachers.

Butter told me, "I won't let Joey push you again. I'll put him in a headlock and make him smell my sweat."

Butter started chugging. And I laughed. Some. At least I wasn't quite so nervous when I went back out to play shortstop.

But the first batter for the Sweepers hit the ball really hard.

The kid who hit it probably could have

gotten a double or a triple. But he stopped at first base.

The Sweepers' coach got after him for that. And the kid said, "I thought I could only go this far."

I don't know why they let guys like that play. He didn't know beans about baseball.

The next guy—a girl—hit a grounder right at me.

I thought of everything. I got my fanny down. And I put my glove on the ground. And I watched the ball.

But the ball bounced sideways. I had to get my fanny up, move it over, and get it down again. And get my glove back on the ground.

I tried to keep my eye on the ball, too. And I sort of did. The ball hit me right on the forehead.

It hurt, too.

But at least the ball dropped on the ground. So I picked it up. And I tossed the ball to second base for the force-out.

Andy caught it. But only for about a second. Then he dropped it.

But the guy on first didn't run to second. Not right away.

Andy picked the ball up. "Step on second," I yelled to him.

Andy looked at me like I was weird or something. But he stepped on second.

And we had one out.

It was great. The coach yelled, "Way to go, Brad. Way to stay in front of the ball."

But Joey yelled, "That's the first time you ever used your head, *Stinkle.*"

And all the guys on the Rug Bugs laughed.

My head was still hurting pretty bad, too. I rubbed it, and I think maybe some tears came to my eyes. Partly because of my head. And partly because of Joey.

But later in the game, Joey played shortstop, and he didn't do any better. Once, a ball bounced right off his glove.

And once, he struck out, the same as me.

Well, not exactly the same. I struck out four times.

Butter never struck out. He hit two homers and a triple and a double.

He never once had his chin against his shoulder. Or his weight on his back foot. Or his head in the game.

He did everything *wrong*. But he hit the ball about three miles every time.

He caught a pop-up without using two hands. And he didn't remember to call for the ball or anything. The only thing he did was reach up and catch it.

I told him about using two hands. I said, "That's what the books say to do."

He only said, "You can't catch a ball with a book."

I was starting to think he was right.

We won the game. Easy. 26–14. But on the way home, in the car, I almost cried.

I'm not a crybaby. But I always thought . I was going to be a good baseball player. And Dad always said I would be.

But I was one of the worst players.

Maybe even *the* worst.

Mom told me, "Brad, it takes a while to learn baseball skills."

And Dad said, "You have to pay the

price, son. Baseball takes a lot of hard work."

I knew he was disappointed in me, though. I could tell by his voice.

But then he said, "Brad, don't worry. Tomorrow, I'll take you to practice on a batting machine. We'll keep working together until you can *crunch* that ball."

That *did* sound like a good idea. But I didn't say so. I was afraid Dad would figure out that I was almost crying.

The next day, when Dad came home, we went to the sports center.

Boy, the batting machine throws *fast.*

Every time I got my stance ready—*thump!* The ball would smack the pad behind me. Then I would swing.

Dad said my timing was off. And I was standing back too far. And stepping away.

But I didn't want to get hit by a ball

that was coming so fast.

So Dad got behind me. He put his arms around me. And he held the bat— with his hands over mine.

All of a sudden, I started knocking the ball hard.

I didn't back up anymore. And I got my timing right.

Boy, I started cracking that ball all over the place.

When the machine ran out of balls, Dad wanted to put more money in. So I could try again by myself.

But I said, "I can do it now, Dad. I just needed to get my timing right."

He thought about that. Then he said, "Maybe so. But we'll come again. We'll keep working on it."

That night, in bed, I remembered how it felt when my bat hit the ball—*crack*.

And I could feel Dad's hands over mine. And his arms around me.

All I had to do was swing the way the two of us had swung together. Then I'd

definitely hit some dingers.

I couldn't wait until the next game.

I was going to get my first hit that wasn't a ticker.

But when the game came, I struck out.

It was in the first inning. We were playing the Nate's Lumber and Hardware Rulers. They were a good team.

"The Rulers rule," they kept yelling.

After I struck out, the catcher told me, "Kid, you swing like my baby sister."

And Joey yelled, "Stinkle can't hit *nothing.*"

The trouble was, he was right.

I didn't cry, but I went to the end of the bench. I sat by myself.

Dad was yelling stuff. So was the coach. And so was Mom. Even Angela was saying, "It's okay, Brad." I guess she felt sorry for me.

But I was thinking I might try soccer
and not play baseball anymore.

Butter was up.

He hit the ball about *ten* miles this time. And I was glad for him. But I didn't go out to home plate.

I got up to bat twice more in the game. And I struck out twice more. Butter got two more good hits.

In the field, I made one good play. I covered second, and Carl threw me the ball. I caught it for a force-out.

But I made a bad play after that. I called for a pop fly, and I held up two hands. But the ball dropped behind me.

After that inning, in the dugout, Joey said, "I'm a better shortstop than you, Stinkle. Lots better."

I didn't say anything. But Butter

walked up to Joey and said, "You better lay off, Doggy-Doo."

"Get out of my way, Butterball."

Just when I thought there was going to be a fight, the coach walked over. "Duden," he said, "I don't want to hear any more of that stuff from you."

"Butter just called me a—" Joey started to say.

But the coach said, "I know who starts things. And don't say different. If I hear it again, you're going to be picking up slivers in your backside—riding the bench."

Joey looked like he just got hit with a pitch.

"Kids on the same team are supposed to pull for each other. But you're on Brad's back all the time," the coach said. "I won't put up with any more of it."

Then he walked away.

Joey turned around and kicked the fence. And he said some words my mom told me never to say.

Butter started to chug like a runaway train.

But I didn't laugh at all. I still felt too rotten.

Something else was bad, too. The Rulers had twelve runs. We only had ten.

And time was running out. The rule was that we played for one hour and then finished the inning we were playing. So this inning was our last chance.

I didn't want to lose. But I also didn't want to get up again. I was afraid I would strike out one more time.

Albert was first up, and he got a hit. A single. That was about the first time he ever got on base.

But then Jeremy made an out.

Joey was up after that. I said, "Come on, Joey. Get a hit." I wanted to be a good sport. And pull for the guys on my team.

He did get a hit, too. He hit a grounder that bounced up and hit the second baseman in the chest.

The kid started rubbing his chest and didn't go after the ball. So we had two on.

That meant Sherry had to get a homer. Then we would win, and I wouldn't have to bat.

The only trouble was, Sherry struck out.

Now there were two outs.

And I was up. It was almost like that time when I hit a homer when my backyard was Yankee Stadium. But this time the ball would be real. I had to do more than just *think* a good hit.

And if I struck out, we would lose.

I walked to the batter's box.

But then one of the kids on the Rulers yelled, "This kid can't hit. Come way in."

That's when I called time-out. I walked back to Butter. He was out of the dugout, on deck.

I had to get some kind of a hit. Even a ticker hit. Then Butter could knock one of his dingers, and we would win.

Butter was wearing his big shirt. I

could see where his mom had taken
COACH off the front and put on RUG BUGS.

I looked at that because I didn't want
to look at his face. I might have had some
tears in my eyes. I'm not sure.

I said, "Butter, tell me again. How do
you get your hits?"

"I just watch for the ball. Then I whack
it," he told me.

So I asked, "Don't you keep your
weight on your back foot and stride forward?"

"I don't know. I just look at the ball.
Then I whack it."

"Do you think I should try that?"

"It works for me."

The umpire was yelling for me to
come back. So I walked to the batter's box
again. I started to get into my stance.

Then I stopped.

I just stood sort of straight. The way Butter does.

At least I didn't feel like I was going to fall down.

Then the coach pitched the ball.

I looked at it. It was a good one. So I whacked it.

I mean, I *really* whacked it. Clear over the outfielders' heads.

Then I took off running as hard as I could.

The Rulers chased after the ball way out in center field.

By the time they got to it, I was going around second, heading for third. Fast!

One of the Rulers threw the ball to the second baseman. By then, I was on my way home.

The second baseman threw to home plate. But he was way too late. I had

already crossed the plate.

I had knocked myself a three-run *dinger!* A real one!

I looked over at the bleachers, and my mom and dad were acting like crazy people—jumping all over the place. Angela was even jumping up and down.

Butter's mom was making siren noises. "Waaaayyyyyyy to gooooooooo, Braaaaaaaaaaaaaaad!"

And Bother was shouting, "Yay, Bwad!"

Coach Moosman yelled, "You won the game! You won the game!"

He hugged me against his big, hairy stomach.

That was the worst part.

I sort of hoped the players might carry me off on their shoulders. But a lot of them hadn't been watching. The girls were fighting with the boys about something.

But Butter grabbed me and lifted me up in the air. And *he* carried me off the field. He was yelling, "I knew you could do it, Brad!"

My mom and dad and little sister were *still* yelling and cheering. And I think Mom was crying. She's kind of a crybaby.

"You're a hero!" Dad told me. "You're going to be a superstar someday. A major leaguer."

I looked at Butter, and he had both his thumbs up. "That's right," he said. He chugged and I laughed.

After the game, we all went out for ice cream: Mom and Dad and Angela and me, and Butter, his mom, and Bother.

Dad bought us anything we wanted.

Butter and I had "hog heaven" banana splits. Only a hog can eat the whole thing. That's what my dad said.

Then he started making noises like a pig.

Butter thought that was pretty funny. But Mom told Dad, "Be quiet, for heaven's sake. People are looking at us."

Dad didn't care. He was too happy. The two of us and Butter laughed until everyone in the place looked.

Butter almost finished his banana split. I could only eat about half of mine.

After we finished, Dad said, "See, Brad, all that practice finally paid off. You're getting the idea now."

"But I didn't do it the way you told me," I told him.

"*What?*"

"I didn't do what you said. Or Coach Moosman. Or the books."

"What did you do?"

"I did what Butter told me. I looked at the ball. Then I *whacked* it."

Butter grinned. "It works for me," he said.

At that, his mom laughed and said, "Thaaaaaat's my booooooyyyyyy."

"Butta's the best pwayer," Bother said.

My mom poked my dad with her elbow. "Butter's a better coach than you are," she said.

My dad laughed. "I think you're right," he said. "But Brad's a natural. He got his talent from me."

"I hope I can be as good as you some-day," I told Dad.

He put his arm around me then and hugged me really hard. Then he said, "You'll be better. You've got Butter for a coach."

But I said, "Will you still help me, though?"

"Sure I will," he said.

So now, I don't get so nervous when I play. I only strike out once or twice in each game. And sometimes I get a good hit.

I also try to keep my eye on the ball when I play shortstop. Sometimes I catch it, and sometimes I don't.

But I'm not the worst player on the team. I'm kind of good and kind of bad. And I'm getting better.

I still want to play in the major leagues someday. Either that or train animals in a circus. Or maybe be a computer guy.

Mostly, I want to work at the same place where Butter works. We're buddies forever. And the Rug Bugs are the best. We've won all our games—except for four—so far.

Joey doesn't call me Stinkle anymore. We're not exactly good friends, but he's not such a bad guy most of the time. He does okay in right field, too.

But my best friend will always be
Butter. He says, "We're Brad and Butter.
We stick together."

And that's right. We do.

About the Author

Dean Hughes has always loved sports. When he was growing up, he played baseball and football and ran on the school track team. "But I was never a star at sports," Dean says. "I found out fairly early that my greater talent was writing." Nowadays, Dean prefers playing golf and *watching* sports, as well as reading, traveling, and, of course, writing. He did run in a marathon once, but says, "I set a goal never to run another one, and so far I've achieved that goal."

Dean Hughes has written over 60 books for children. He's best known for his *Angel Park* sports series. He makes his home in Utah with his wife, and has three children and three grandchildren.

About the Illustrator

"I really enjoyed illustrating *Brad and Butter Play Ball!* I played little league baseball as a kid, and now my son Brett plays. We have both experienced difficulties and triumphs on the baseball field, just like Brad."

Born and raised in Houston, Layne Johnson has been a successful artist for 15 years. He lives in Houston with his wife and son.